Mum
Grandma
Baby Sid
Flo
Grandpa

This book is dedicated to
Jack, Felipe, Ella, Millie and Harrie

EGMONT
*We bring stories to life*

First published in Great Britain in 2014
by Egmont UK Limited
The Yellow Building, 1 Nicholas Road, London W11 4AN
www.egmont.co.uk



ISBN 978 1 4052 6821 9

A CIP catalogue record for this book is available from the British Library.

# the funny fingers

Nikalas Catlow, David Sinden & Matthew Morgan

EGMONT

The Funny Fingers were an unusual family but a very happy one. They loved to have fun.

Mum and Dad had fun decorating the house.

"Ha ha, how about a blue and yellow floor?" Mum asked.

"Yippee!" Dad replied. "Blue like the sky and yellow like bananas!"

Grandpa and Grandma had fun roller skating along the hallway.

"Wheeeee!" said Grandpa, waving his stick.

Grandma laughed, "Whoop! Whoop!"

Finn and Flo had fun dressing up.

"Let's sail away on a sea of bubbles!" Flo said.

"Off we go with a yo-ho-ho!" said Finn.

"Tee-hee! Don't forget me!"
Baby Sid chuckled.
He was having fun being
a fearsome shark.

Laughter could always be heard ringing out from the Funny Fingers' house.

"Ha ha!"

"Wahey!"

"Wheeeeee!"

"Tee-hee!"

"Yo-ho-ho!"

"Whoop! Whoop!"

"Yippee!"

But not everyone enjoyed the sound . . .

Next door lived two Terrible Toes.

“Those Funny Fingers are having fun again,” Mrs Toe grumbled.

“I don’t like fun,” Mr Toe complained. “Let’s make them STOP!”

The Terrible Toes crept to the Funny Fingers' house, each with a handful of toe cheese.

"Ready?" Mr Toe whispered.

The toes took aim . . .

SPLAT! SPLAT! SPLAT!

The toes threw
in the cheese.

But the Funny Fingers,
seeing one another
splattered, just laughed
even more.

"Bother,"
Mrs Toe said
crossly.

"Hee
hee!"

"Ha ha!"

"I've got another idea," Mr Toe said. He climbed up to the roof and poked a hosepipe down the chimney.

Mrs Toe turned the water on . . .

The Funny Fingers' house began filling up with water! But they even found that fun, too!

"I'm swimming like a mermaid," said Flo.

"Anyone for scuba diving?" Dad bubbled.

The Terrible Toes grumped home and peered into a hut in their garden where Errol, their pet foot monster, lived.

"Errol, wake up you filthy beast! We need you to pay those Funny Fingers a visit . . ."

Errol the foot monster hopped to the Funny Fingers' house and barged in.

"GRRRRRRR!" he growled.

"AAARGH!" shrieked the Funny Fingers.

"RUN!"
"Let's get out of here!"
"Uh-oh!"

But even escaping from a foot monster was fun for the Funny Fingers. They sped off in their car with Errol in pursuit.

"Full speed ahead!" cried Mum.

They reached a lake and leapt into a boat.

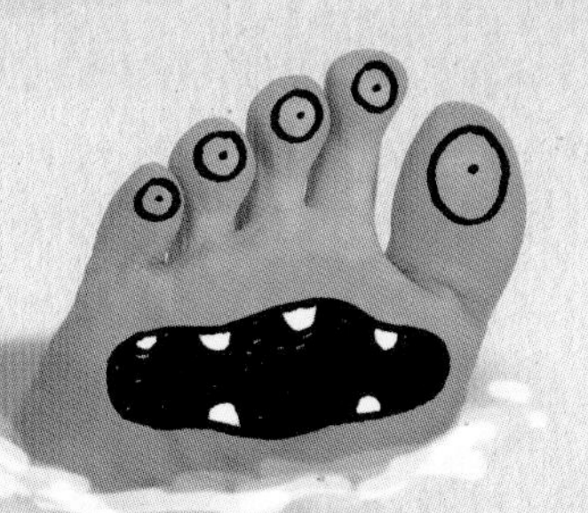

“Row, row, row, with a yo-ho-ho!” Finn cheered, as they paddled across the water.

They boarded a train,

then a rollercoaster . . .

but still Errol kept chasing them.

"Escaping is so much fun!" Grandma beamed, as the Funny Fingers floated away in a hot-air balloon, just out of the reach of the foot monster.

Or so they thought . . .

"He's still after us!" Dad called.

The Funny Fingers held on tightly as the wind blew them back towards their house.

"Look, I can see the Terrible Toes in their garden," said Flo.

Grandpa had an idea. "Let's drop in to say hello. Parachutes on, everyone!" He poked the balloon with his walking stick . . .

POP
The balloon burst.

The Funny Fingers opened their parachutes and floated down gently.

Errol didn't have a parachute. He tumbled and whirled until he landed with a bump on top of . . .

. . . the Terrible Toes!
“Errol, get off, you oaf!”
Mr Toe grumped.

But just as Errol was about to move, the Funny Fingers landed and started tickling him to make him laugh!

Soon everyone was giggling and having fun.
Well, almost everyone . . .

"Ha ha! Ha ha!
Ha ha haaaaa!"

"STOP!" the toes demanded.
"Please stop having FUN!"

But the Funny Fingers never did because . . .

Fingers just love to have fun!
Ha ha, hee hee, ho ho!

"Yippee!"
"Yo-ho-ho!"
"Tee-hee!"
BEWARE

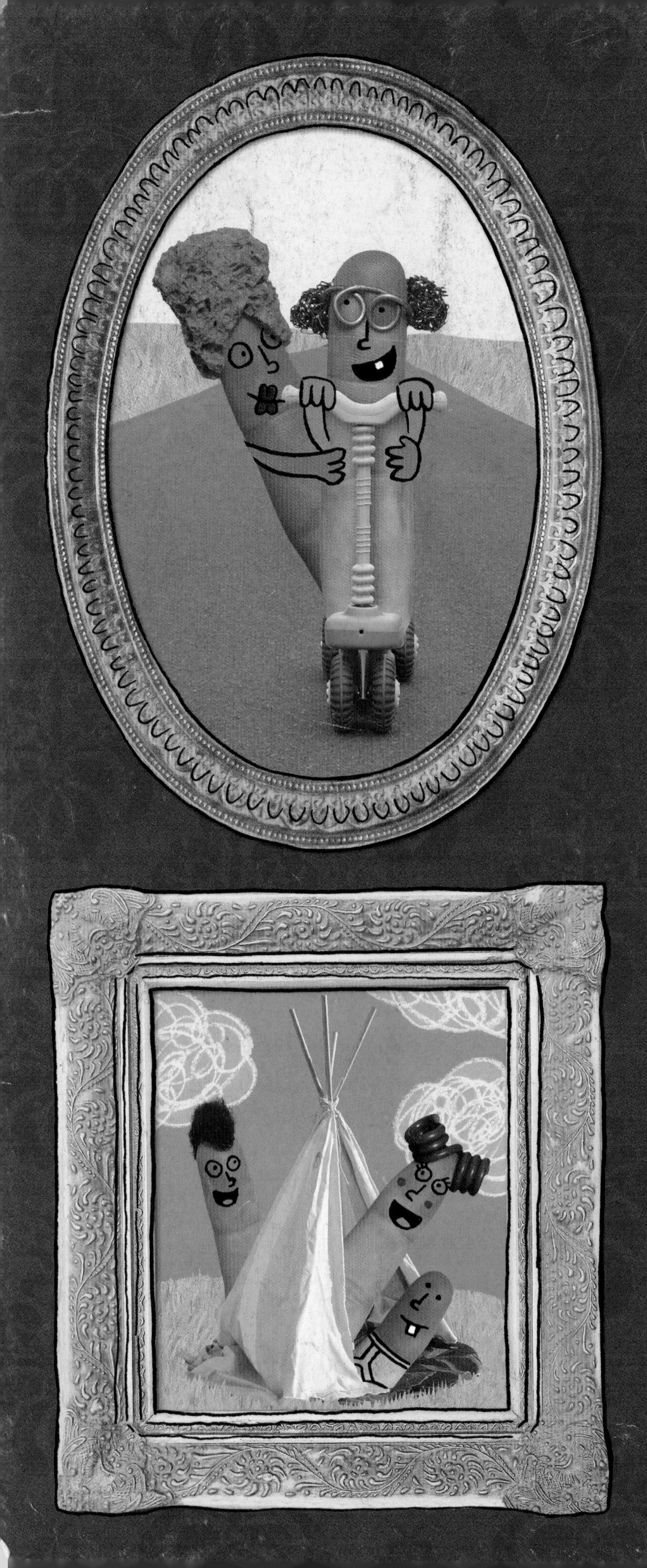

Errol
The Terrible Toes